Superfairies

Martha the Little Mouse

by Janey Louise Jones

illustrated by Jennie Poh

PICTURE WINDOW BOOKS

a capstone imprint

Superfairies is published by Picture Window Books
A Capstone Imprint
1710 Roe Crest Drive
North Mankato, Minnesota 56003
www.mycapstone.com

Text © 2016 Janey Louise Jones
Illustrations © 2016 Jennie Poh

Library of Congress Cataloging-in-Publication Data

Jones, Janey, 1968- author.
  Martha the little mouse / by Janey Louise Jones;
illustrated by Jennie Poh.
        pages cm. -- (Superfairies)
  Summary: When the Autumn Queen ushers in a big
storm, and little Martha Mouse is swept away by the
big wind, it is up to the Superfairies to rescue her.
  ISBN 978-1-4795-8643-1 (library binding) -- ISBN
978-1-4795-8647-9 (pbk.) -- ISBN 978-1-4795-8651-
6 (ebook pdf)
1. Mice--Juvenile fiction. 2. Fairies--Juvenile fiction.
3. Rescues--Juvenile fiction. 4. Autumn--Juvenile
fiction. [1. Mice--Fiction. 2. Fairies--Fiction. 3.
Rescues--Fiction. 4. Autumn--Fiction.] I. Poh, Jennie,
illustrator. II. Title.
  PZ7.J72019Mar 2016
  [E]--dc23
                                    2015031706

Designer: Alison Thiele

For Karen, the brightest star
– Jennie Poh

Printed and bound in US.
007522CGS16

Table of Contents

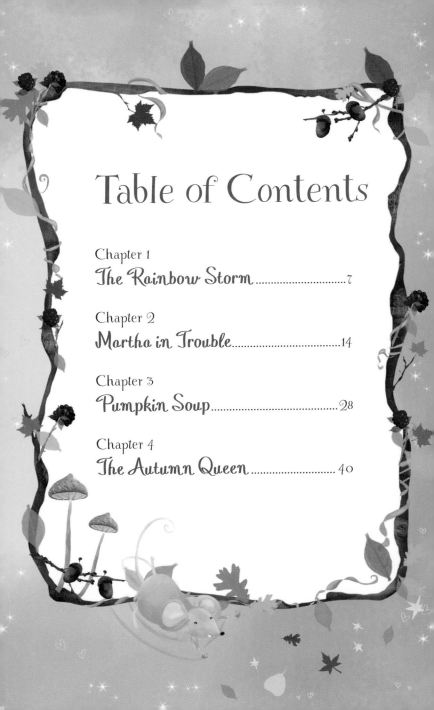

The Fairy World

The Superfairies of Peaseblossom Woods use
teamwork to rescue animals in trouble. They
bring together their special superskills,
petal power, and lots of love.

Superfairy Rose
can blow super healing fairy
kisses to make the animals in
Peaseblossom Woods feel better.

Superfairy Berry can see for miles around with her super eyesight.

Superfairy Star can create super dazzling brightness in one dainty spin to lighten up dark places.

Superfairy Silk spins super strong webs for animal rescues.

Chapter 1

The Rainbow Storm

Superfairy Rose was busy in the
cherry blossom tree making a skirt from
golden autumn leaves.

Meanwhile, out in the woods, Martha
the Little Mouse and Susie Squirrel held
hands and danced around in circles under
the big oak tree. It had been raining
heavily all morning and now a huge
rainbow was in the sky.

"It's quite sunny now. Shall we go off on an adventure?" suggested Martha.

"I'm not sure," said Susie Squirrel. "Mom and Dad said there's going to be an autumn storm later."

"How could there be a storm when the sun is shining?" giggled Martha. "Grown-ups exaggerate. Let's explore!"

The girls set off along the woodland floor, looking for somewhere to play.

They heard familiar voices. "That's Basil the Bear Cub and my brother Sidney!" said Susie. "Let's see what they're up to!"

The girls teamed up with the boys and chased each other through the woods.

"Autumn is so pretty!" said Martha. "I love the golden leaves and all the berries and fruits!"

But before long, raindrops fell through the copper-colored trees.

Plink! Splash! Splatter!

The rain got heavier very quickly. It spilled onto the carpet of leaves as if a faucet had been turned on.

Crackle! Splish! Splosh!

A cold wind whipped angrily through the woods.

Whoosh! Swish! Flap!

The sky became very dark.

"What happened to the sun?" said Martha.

"It looks like the sky is frowning!" cried Basil Bear.

Martha looked up. "Oh, look! It's the Autumn Queen flying over the woods!"

"Yes," said Sidney. "She's bringing a big storm with her!"

"Oh, she's beautiful!" gasped Martha. "But I'm scared. Why does she have to bring such an angry storm every autumn?"

"Because she needs to shake off all the leaves for winter!" explained Basil.

"The trees have to sleep while we do. And while they're sleeping, the new buds of spring start to grow. They couldn't be green all year—they would run out of energy. That's what my Dad told me. And he knows everything."

"I wish it could just be summer all year!" said Martha. "I love sunshine."

"That would be boring," said Basil. "I love storms! This is exciting!"

"I don't like it. I'm going home now," said Martha. "I want to be safe and cozy with Mom and Dad."

All the young animals began to scuttle back to their families for shelter and food.

"See you later, Martha," called Susie, as she went off in the opposite direction of her best friend.

Chapter 2

Martha in Trouble

That night, as the Superfairies snuggled into their cozy beds in the cherry blossom tree, the wild storm raged around them.

"Oh, I hate storms!" said Rose as the wind howled and whistled, making the whole blossom tree sway in the wind.

"It should be over by morning," said Star.

"Goodnight, everyone!" called Silk.

"Goodnight!" said all the Superfairies.

But—

Ting-aling-aling...

Ting-aling-aling...

"Oh, the animals need us!" cried Rose.
"I will have to be brave for them."

Rose took courage from the other
fairies. They wrapped up warmly in their
autumn cloaks. Then they flew out through
the wind and rain to the fairycopter. They
climbed inside.

"Rose, what does the Strawberry computer show?" asked Star.

"It's the poor little mice!" said Rose. She examined her computer screen. "The wind has blown the roof off the Mousey House. They're freezing!"

"Hurry up. We can bring the mice back to the cherry blossom tree in the fairycopter and make them cozy here for the night!" suggested Silk.

"Yes, we have plenty of space for them. We'll give them pumpkin soup and hot chocolate, and iced gingerbread," said Rose.

"This could be a bumpy ride," said Berry as she started up the fairycopter.

The other three Superfairies held hands.

"Ready for take-off!" announced Berry. "5, 4, 3, 2, 1 ... go, go, go!"

Berry used her super eyesight to steer the fairycopter safely through the storm, but it was choppy.

The fairycopter fluttered to the east ... and to the west ... to the north ... and to the south. But Berry managed to steer back on course, using the big gusts of wind to power them.

They soon landed in front of the Mousey House with a tremble, a bump, and a thud!

The whole Mouse family was huddled together in a corner of the roofless house.

"Thank goodness you've arrived!" said Mr. Mouse.

Little Martha was delighted to see the Superfairies. She ran towards the fairycopter excitedly.

"No, Martha! The wind's too strong. Stay in here," called her mother.

But Martha was already out on the woodland floor.

"Thanks for coming, Superfairies!" said Martha. "I hate storms!"

But with that—whoooossssh! A gust of wind whisked the dainty mouse into the air and twirled her around wildly between the branches.

"Oh, my baby!" cried Mr. Mouse.

They all watched helplessly as Martha began to ...

spin

twist

tumble

and twirl

She flapped around the treetops with the autumn leaves circling her.

"Superfairies to the rescue!" cried Rose, finding her own courage at last. She flew from the fairycopter out into the windy woods.

The fairies held hands and fought against the wind as they fluttered towards Martha.

But as they got close to her, a fresh blast of wind swirled the feather-light little mouse off in the opposite direction.

"Help me!" cried Martha, as she was whisked out of reach.

"We'll save you!" called Silk.

Martha was carried in the air through the woods. As the Superfairies and Mouse family followed her, the other animals in the woods became concerned too.

The Squirrel family watched Martha twirl over the treetops. They were so worried that they got too close to the edge of their nest. It tipped up, falling down from their tree! Down the squirrels fell with it.

Bump! The nest and squirrels landed on the woodland floor.

All the squirrels were a bit shaken up by the fall.

"Are you all right?" called Rose.

"Yes, we're fine," said Mr. Squirrel.

However, Susie Squirrel, who was best friends with Martha, got very upset indeed to see her friend twirling about the treetops. She began to sob.

"I will climb to the top of the tallest tree and try to reach over to Martha!" she said.

"No!" cried Berry. "It's too dangerous! Stay with your parents, Susie!"

But the little squirrel set off regardless, longing to feel useful.

She scurried to the top of a huge oak tree and held onto a curving branch. She leaned out over the wood, stretching as far as she could towards her best friend.

The Superfairies hovered between Martha and Susie.

Susie was determined to take hold of her friend.

"Take my hand, Martha," she called as the little mouse continued to flap around the sky between the trees. "Pleeeeeease."

Martha tried to reach Susie.

Their arms were outstretched towards each other.

They nearly touched.

Almost. But not quite.

The Superfairies gathered round Martha, trying to scoop her in their arms.

"I'm so tired!" called Martha.

"We're doing all we can," said Rose. She blew healing kisses at the little mouse.

There was a brief break in the gusts of wind, so Martha dropped down below the treetops, where it was more sheltered.

The Superfairies managed to gather around Martha now.

"Stay in close to her," advised Star.

The fairies guided Martha towards the branch Susie was on.

"Come on, Martha, you can do it," said Susie. "You'll soon be safe and cozy if you just reach over to me."

With Susie's sweet voice in Martha's ears and the Superfairies guiding her, she finally made it to the branch of the tree!

Chapter 3

Pumpkin Soup

"Hold on, Martha," cried Star.

"Hooray!" cried all the animals on the woodland floor below.

The Mouse family danced around in a circle.

"Wait on this branch," said Berry, "and I will go and get the fairycopter. Then you girls can hop in."

"Yay, we get to ride in the fairycopter!" said Susie, hugging her friend excitedly.

They wobbled on the branch.

"Whoa!" said Susie. "We don't want to fall off, do we?"

"Exactly," said Rose, "so be very still and careful until Berry arrives!"

Silk called to the animals below. "Everyone, make your way to our cherry blossom tree, but hold hands as you go. And be very careful of the wind! Just go in and put some logs on the fire!"

The Superfairies helped Martha and Susie into the fairycopter. Berry flew everyone back to the cherry blossom tree.

"Phew! I'm exhausted!" said Berry as she landed the fairycopter. "That was quite a rescue!"

"I know," agreed Rose. "Wasn't Susie wonderful? Let's heat some soup, warm some bread, and sit around the fire, shall we?"

"Yes," agreed Berry. "That sounds lovely."

The rest of the mice and squirrels were already in the sitting room, toasting their toes.

The Superfairies got busy warming up pumpkin soup, icing gingerbread, whisking hot chocolate, and toasting marshmallows.

The strong winds raged around the tree house.

Once everyone was served, Rose sat very quietly, listening for the bells, just in case.

She looked deep in thought.

"What are you thinking about?" asked Silk.

"About how much harm this storm is causing," said Rose. "And what we can do about it."

The Superfairies invited the animals to stay overnight with them. "Make yourselves at home," said Star.

Meanwhile, Rose called a meeting of the Superfairies.

"What's wrong?" asked Berry as they gathered around the kitchen table.

"I think we should all go to see the Autumn Queen now," said Rose.

"Why?" asked Berry.

"Yes, what for?" wondered Star.

"We need to tell her that this storm is hurting the animals. She will understand," said Rose.

The Superfairies decided there was no
time to waste.

"Shall we wear our formal cloaks?"
asked Berry.

"Of course," said Rose. "We must
show our respect to the great queen. We
should not anger her in any way."

Rose continued. "We need to find her kindness. It colors the woods with gold and bronze and copper. It ripens the harvest so we can eat in the winter. I know it's there."

The Superfairies tucked the animals into bed with hot chocolate.

"We have some work to do," explained Rose. "But you rest well and let us hope the woods are calmer by morning."

"Goodnight—and thank you!" said Mrs. Mouse. She held Martha close to her as they snuggled up for the night in one of the Superfairies' spare flower beds.

The fairies then brushed each other's hair until it was smooth and shiny. They dressed for their important visit to the Autumn Queen's Corner.

Rose wore a silver cloak and her silver crown.

Star wore a golden cloak and her golden crown.

Silk wore a lilac cloak and her lilac crown.

Berry wore a ruby red cloak and her ruby red crown.

Rose led the way as they held hands and flitter-fluttered through the swaying trees in search of the powerful Autumn Queen.

The leaves from the beautiful trees of Peaseblossom Woods floated around them like golden confetti.

The fierce winds were not calming and the rains still fell. Rose knew they were doing the right thing. If only they could find the beautiful Autumn Queen, Rose felt sure they could ask her to calm the storm.

"This looks familiar!" said Star as they arrived at an enchanting corner of the woods. They entered a pathway leading to the secret fairy throne room.

Gold and silver tree branches arched over the pathway. It was perfectly calm and sheltered. There were glowing lanterns hanging in the branches that lit the way to the throne room.

"I always forget how beautiful it is!" whispered Berry.

They arrived at the entrance and looked in.

A vast throne of twisted twigs and bronze leaves sat in the middle of the room.

But the Autumn Queen was not on her throne.

"Where is she?" whispered Berry.

"She will appear," said Rose. "I know it."

Nothing happened. The fairies hovered.

"She cannot be rushed," said Silk. "She's super busy as it is her own season."

Rose nodded.

After a few moments, the Superfairies heard a rustling of leaves.

They blinked and the beautiful Autumn Queen magically appeared on her throne!

Chapter 4

The Autumn Queen

She was majestic. Her long hair gleamed and her golden gown sparkled. A crown of branches framed her pretty face. The Superfairies bowed before her.

Rose moved a little closer to the queen.

"We are sorry to trouble you," said Rose.

"I know why you've come, and I'm sorry about the storm," said the Autumn Queen. "But it's my job to make the trees ready for their winter sleep. I send the winds to bring down the leaves and sometimes they get rather wild."

"Yes, of course," said Rose. "But the animals are suffering."

"I send the rain to make sure there is plenty of water to drink in winter," the queen explained. "I try my best to think of what the animals will need in the cold months."

The queen added, "But I don't want to cause suffering. I love the animals as you do."

"We know that," said Berry, stepping forward. "But we had to rescue Martha today after the wind picked her up. We very nearly lost her."

"Oh, that's terrible," said the queen. "Let me work some magic..."

"Thank you," said the Superfairies.

"You do very important work here in the woods," said the queen, "and we are all grateful for it."

"It is our pleasure," said Silk. "We work with the seasons, not against them."

The Autumn Queen smiled kindly, then nodded her head to show the Superfairies that they should leave.

They flew back a different way. They followed the lines of the river, listening to owls hooting as they went.

By the time they got back to the cherry blossom tree, the storm was starting to calm.

"Ssssh," said Rose. "The animals will be sleeping."

The Superfairies crept into the house.

"Surprise!" cried Martha and Susie. "We couldn't sleep so we thought we'd have an autumn party!"

"Oh, how lovely," said Rose.

The Superfairies giggled.

"Great surprise," said Berry. "Is that the pumpkin soup I smell?"

"Yes!" said Susie. "And more iced gingerbread!"

Rose went to lock the big door. She looked outside. The night sky twinkled with bright stars.

"Hey, everyone," she called. "Looks like the storm has passed over."

"Hooray!" said Martha, dancing. "No more winds!"

"Let's gather around the fire now," said Rose, "and sing songs!"

"Yeah!" cried Star. "And I know just the song to start with!"

Fairies from the blossom tree,
Superskills galore have we.

Caring in this charming wood
For needy animals, as we should.

Twinkle, sparkle, dazzle, swish,
Tending animals as they wish.

And when a rescue's nicely done,
It's time to have some fairy fun.

Dancing, singing, twirling, glee,
All around our blossom tree!

Glossary

adventure (ad-VEN-chur)—an exciting or unusual experience

confetti (kuhn-FET-ee)—tiny pieces of paper thrown at weddings

exaggerate (eg-ZAJ-uh-rate)—make something sound larger, better, or worse than it is

formal (FOR-muhl)—serious

majestic (muh-JESS-tik)—having impressive beauty

scuttle (SKUH-tuhl)—run in a hurry

snuggle (SNUHG-uhl)—settle into a warm and comfortable position

swirl (SWURL)—move in twisting patterns

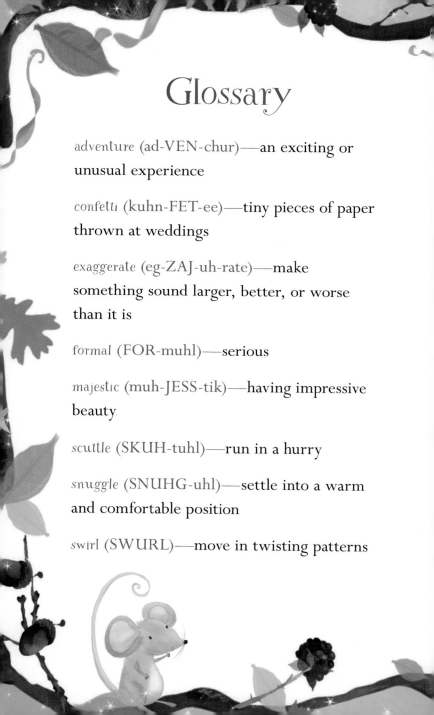

Talk It Out

1. Do you like autumn? Think about the weather, nature, foods, and traditions.

2. Martha and Susie are best friends, so Susie is worried about Martha. What ways do you show your friends that you care?

3. If you were going dress up as an Autumn Queen using things from nature, what would you need?

Write It Down

1. Design an invitation to an autumn theme party!

2. Write a short letter to the Autumn Queen explaining how the storm is hurting the animals.

3. Write an e-mail from the Autumn Queen to the Winter Queen, telling her what is happening in the autumn season.

All About Fairies

The legend of fairies is as old as time. Fairy tales tell stories of fairy magic. According to legend, fairies are so small and delicate, and fly so fast, that they might actually be all around us, but just very hard to see. Fairies, supposedly, only reveal themselves to believers.

Fairies often dance in circles at sunrise and sunset. They love to play in woodlands among wildflowers. If you sing gently to them, they may appear.

Here are some of the world's most famous fairies:

The Flower Fairies

Artist Cicely Mary Barker painted a range of pretty flower fairies and published eight volumes of flower fairy art from 1923. The link between fairies and flowers is very strong.

The Tooth Fairy

She visits us during the night to leave a coin when we lose our baby teeth. Although it is very hard to catch sight of her, children are always happy when she visits.

Fake Fairies

In 1917, cousins Elsie Wright and Frances Griffiths said they photographed fairies in their garden. They later admitted that most were fakes—but Frances claimed that one was genuine.

Which Superfairy Are You?

1. Which is your favorite treat?
   A) donut
   B) iced cupcake
   C) strawberry tart
   D) fresh cream meringue

2. Do you prefer:
   A) winter
   B) spring
   C) summer
   D) fall

3. Are you mostly:
   A) energetic
   B) thoughtful
   C) sensible
   D) funny

4. Would you rather:
   A) travel the world
   B) wander in a field of flowers
   C) fly an airplane
   D) dance on stage

5. If it was raining and you couldn't go outside, would you rather:
   A) play board games with a friend
   B) do a jigsaw puzzle
   C) clean your room
   D) dance in your room

6. Do you like to wear:
   A) sneakers
   B) sandals
   C) boots
   D) ballet shoes

7. What is your favorite animal?
   A) lion
   B) giraffe
   C) dog
   D) horse

8. If you were choosing a new dress, would it be:
   A) purple
   B) pink
   C) red
   D) yellow

Mostly A—you are like Silk. Adventurous and brave, you always think of ways to deal with problems! You enjoy action and adventures.

Mostly B—you are like Rose: gentle, kind, and loving. You are good at staying calm and love pink things.

Mostly C—you are like Berry: good fun, always helpful, with lots of great ideas. You are sensible and wise.

Mostly D—you are like Star. You cheer people up and dazzle with your sparkling ways! You are funny and enjoy jokes and dancing.

About the Author

Janey Louise Jones has been a published author for 10 years. Her Princess Poppy series is an international bestselling brand, with books translated into 10 languages, including Hebrew and Mandarin. Janey is a graduate of Edinburgh University and lives in Edinburgh, Scotland with her three sons. She loves fairies, princesses, beaches, and woodlands.

About the Illustrator

Jennie Poh was born in England and grew up in Malaysia (in the jungle). At the age of 10 she moved back to England and trained as a ballet dancer. She studied fine art at Surrey Institute of Art & Design as well as fashion illustration at Central Saint Martins. Jennie loves the countryside, animals, tea, and reading. She lives in Woking, England with her husband and two wonderful daughters.

JOIN THE

Superfairies

ON MORE
MAGICAL
ANIMAL RESCUES!

Basil the Bear Cub
by Janey Louise Jones

Dancer the Wild Pony
by Janey Louise Jones

Martha the Little Mouse
by Janey Louise Jones

Violet the Velvet Rabbit
by Janey Louise Jones

THE *Fun* DOESN'T STOP HERE!

For MORE GREAT BOOKS go to
WWW.MYCAPSTONE.COM